Theodore H. (Theodore Harding) Rand

At Minas Basin

And other Poems

Theodore H. (Theodore Harding) Rand

At Minas Basin
And other Poems

ISBN/EAN: 9783744772020

Printed in Europe, USA, Canada, Australia, Japan

Cover: Foto ©Andreas Hilbeck / pixelio.de

More available books at **www.hansebooks.com**

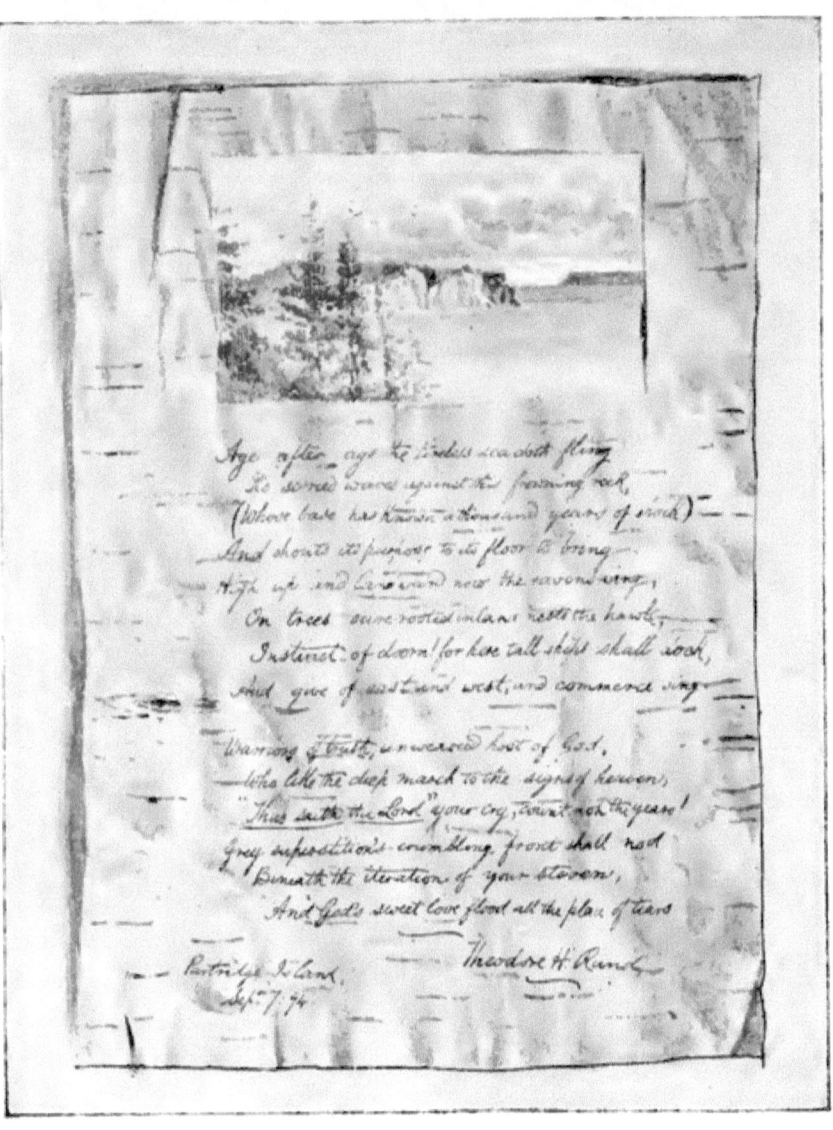

Reduced fac-simile of original of page 34.

AT MINAS BASIN

And Other Poems

BY

THEODORE H. RAND

D. C. L.

TORONTO:

WILLIAM BRIGGS

WESLEY BUILDINGS.

Montreal: C. W. COATES.   Halifax: S. F. HUESTIS.

1897

To E.

SHARER OF PERFECT SUMMER DAYS

AT PARTRIDGE ISLAND

BASIN OF MINAS

TORONTO, CANADA,
1897

A body of beauty is mine.
  O poet, moulder of me,
Withhold not the breath divine,
  The soul of truth that makes free.

Fair form in repose for a day
  (The body of beauty of me)
With the pulse-beats of life all away,
  Is well, for beauty and thee.

Yet give to me life all aglow,—
  Not a demon of darkness to blight,
But a love-lit soul pure as snow,—
  Beckon me an angel of light.

A body of beauty is mine.
  O poet, moulder of me,
Inbreathe with breathings divine,
  Or body alone let it be.

CONTENTS.

B

CONTENTS.

CONTENTS.

CONTENTS.

AT MINAS BASIN.

ABOUT the buried feet of Blomidon,
    Red-breasted sphinx with crown of grey and green,
    The tides of Minas swirl,—their veilèd queen
    Fleet-oared from far by galleys of the sun.
The tidal breeze blows its divinest gale!
    The blue air winks with life like beaded wine!—
    Storied of Glooscap, of Evangeline—
    Each to the setting sun this sea did sail.
Opulent day has poured its living gold
    Till all the west is belt with crimson bars,
    Now darkness lights its silver moon and stars,—
The festal beauty of the world new-old.
    Facing the dawn, in vigil that ne'er sleeps,
    The sphinx the secret of the Basin keeps.

THE RAIN CLOUD.

Swift changed to storm tones is the golden air,
   And shut the heavens with the descending veil
   Of cloud,—here warm and brown, there cold and
       pale,
   White-veined with sudden fire and red with glare.
Now falls the twisted rain, like unbound hair,
   Dusking the wooded hills and mountain trail,
   Now, marshalled by the trumpets of the gale,
   Sweeps wide with level lances to their blare.

O rain cloud, minister of cooling dew
   To waiting harvests sheathed in mystery,
   Bearer of blessed balms for fevered ills !
Thy rending veil breaks on the holiest blue,
   All quick and palpitant as angels see,
   And God's smile falls upon the breathing hills.

THE ROSE.

FIVE-PETALED splendor set in hillside place,
    Parent of queenly sisterhood that stir
    To every garden wind, and swift confer
    Attar to pour from out each precious vase!
Symbol of secrecy to Latin race,
    Virtue and blood to York and Lancaster,
    Thy tint *de Pompadour* sweet arts transfer
    To Sevres', and erst "rose noble" bore thy grace.

To me thou art the glow of secret heat
    That burneth at the heart of day and night,
    An odorous flush of beauty without blame,—
Love's oriel wherethrough my eyes discreet
    May look far in beyond the outward sight
    And, unconsumëd, see His fiery flame.

A WILLOW AT GRAND PRÉ.

THE fitful rustle of thy sea-green leaves
   Tells of the homeward tide, and free-blown air
   Upturns thy gleaming leafage like a share,—
   A silvery foam thy bosom, as it heaves!
O peasant tree, the regal Bay doth bare
   Its throbbing breast to ebbs and floods—and
      grieves!
   O slender fronds, pale as a moonbeam weaves,
   Joy woke your strain that trembles to despair!

Willow of Normandy, say, do the birds
   Of Motherland plain in thy sea-chant low,
   Or voice of those who brought thee in the ships
To tidal vales of Acadie?—Vain words!
   Grief unassuaged makes moan that Gaspereau
   Bore on its flood the fleet with iron lips!

SEA-WIDOWED lands more fair than Tantramar!
   Winter's green providence in July's sun!
   The clattering steel till all was over and done,
   Flashed on thy breast from dawn to evening star.
Soon herds of sweet-breathed kine of sere Canard,
   Whose eager hoofs the hasting morn outrun,
   Sea of lush clover aftermath has won,
   And golden-girdled bees anear and far.

Lo, as the harvest moon comes up the sky,
   Her shield of argent mellowed to the rim,
   The phantom of the buried tide doth flow;
And without noise of wave or sea-bird's cry
   Fills all thy ancient channels to the brim,
   Thy levels of a thousand years ago!

LOVE'S IMMANENCE.

I WATCH the cloud soft-poised in upper air
    And feel a presence bodied in its folds,
    The wind in dark and shine a voice aye holds,
    The noontide forest listens to my prayer.
The trampling seas with rumbling chariots bear
    Significant behests in heats and colds,
    Urim fire throbs intense on barren wolds—
    The crystal globëd dew-drops Love declare!

The silence of the wheeling heavens by night,
    By day, is but the pealing anthem sweet
    Beyond the pitch of my dull ears to hear,
While veiling shadows are the excess of light
    That marks the goings of His power so near,
    And hides Love's regal presence on His seat.

MYSTERY.

O veiled enchantress of my days and nights,
  That in sweet wonder's realm of witchery
  To fairer visions ever beckons me,
  Thou'st left the valleys for the rugged heights !
A gladsome youth, the hill of thy delights
  Winged my lithe spirit to speed after thee,
  But now, come down, close-veiléd Mystery,
  The garish sun but withers and affrights.

I feel thy charm, shy and elusive one,
  As in the gleaming springtide of my life,
  Whose zest was all thy unattained pursuit.
Still flit before me till the race is run,
  And when with doubt the common day is rife,
  Thy wonder-wand set thick with flower and fruit.

THE NIGHT-FISHER.

GREY liegeman of sundown and dawn, who chides
    With a lone song the ocean-murmuring trees,
    I haste with thee at dusk to stalk the seas
    Where feed the finny flocks of shepherding tides.
O wild the pulses beat as round us glides
    The tidal spirit, like a midnight breeze,
    Burdened with moan of life-and-death decrees,—
    The deep night's tide-line pacing with our strides !

More weird than winkings of the ruddy Mars
    These flitting gleams and breaths of hell and
        heaven,
    Searching the shadowy folds 'twixt peace and
        dread !—
Nor dreamed I such solemnities did leaven
    Life's daily meal and league its dole of bread
    With unseen forces vaster than the stars'.

A DEEP-SEA SHELL.

[GEORGE V. DEARBORN.]

ARRIVED from out abysmal deeps of brine,
   A regal splendor glows within thy whorl,
   Like pomp of rosy morn in shimmering pearl.
   Surely "the hand that made thee is divine"!
Ah, why so richly dight for beauty's shrine?
   No eye can feast on walls of gemmëd burl
   Far down the overwhelming rush and swirl
   Of awful wastes scarce plumbed of fathom-line!

Fit for the palace of high seneschal!
   Inlaid with colors which the Tyrian King
   Vain sought to rival on his royal scroll,
And echoing yet the ocean's trembling string:
   Methinks the Master wrought this ivory hall
   To please the love of beauty in His soul.

A RED SUNRISE.

THE naked Bay its silver notes is telling
   Sweeter than flute or harp or singing bird,
   Beatings of rosy rhythm in winsome word
   Of lilting song are softly shoreward welling:
Anear and far the ruddy waters swelling,
   In laughter-peals around the fair earth heard,
   Thrill swift the home-bound keels so long un-
      stirred—
   The kiss of day the weary wings compelling.

Beware the elfin bugles sounding clear
   As glows morn's pallid ash to crimson flame
   And makes a bloody dazzle of the waves!
Ere burn the embers in the west all blear,
   The deep shall thunder its awful chant of fame
   O'er noble hearts gone down to wandering graves.

THE opal fires are gone, and but a stain
   Of day yet lingers as the sudden night
   With swift cloud blots the crouching hills from
      sight,
   And the far sea moans deep in ominous pain.
Ah me, it is the swart-winged hurricane !
   The furious tide in elemental fight
   Is lashing fierce and hoar with giant might,—
   The bleeding shores the tale shall tell the main !

Brave sailor, reeling in thy storm-drunk bark,
   Blinded by sheeted rain blown tempest-wild,
   And vexed with roaring darkness round about !
The heaven-sent vision fair of wife and child
   Calm seated at love's hearth, with face ahark,
   Makes thee divine amid the awful rout.

THE CUMULUS CLOUD.

MOUNTAINS of heaven, in stainless white ye shine,
   Islanded in calm of pearl- and sapphire-blue !
   The pillared heights are lifted into view
   In spectral power reposeful as divine.
A timeless peace abides in every line
   Soft moulded from the quarries of the dew,
   Yet fateful fire the inmost heart throbs through,
   And thunder slumbers in the brows benign.

Paling before the massive whiteness there,
   The faltering moon comes up the waiting night ;
   The faithful stars, like folded lilies, sleep
Till Love's wide wonder of the lullëd air
   Melts with its rose-tipt crests in azure deep,
   And sets the skyey plains abloom with light.

SEA FOG.

HERE danced an hour ago a sapphire sea;
  Now, airy nothingness, wan spaces vast,
  Pale draperies of the formless fog o'ercast,
  And wreathëd waters grey with mystery!
The ship glides like a phantom silently,
  As screams the white-winged gull before the mast;
  Weird elemental shapes go flitting past,
  Which loom as giant ghosts above the quay.

The vapor lifts!   Again the sea gleams bright;
  The heavens have hid within their chambers far
  Cloud-stuff of gossamer, from which are spun
To-morrow's skyey pomps inwove with light,
  The belted splendors for the rising sun,
  And rosy curtains for the evening star.

PARTRIDGE ISLAND.

THE title deeds of these rich shores are thine
   By age,—thine, too, by succor and defence;
   Ere they were kissed by winds, or waves beat
      thence,
   Thy breast of beauty broke the beating brine.
All hail, fair Isle, first born! Thy jeweled shrine
   Is worn by pilgrim feet; thy firgroves dense,
   Peopled with Hamadryads, cheat the sense
   With frolic fays and all the rosy Nine.

These younglings—Gilbert's Cliff, and Sharp, and
      Split,
   Bold Silver Crag, the Islands Five, and Two,
   And broad-browed Blomidon—the Basin's Ben,—
When comes the witchery of fog-wreathed view,
   Each robed in richest hues, with curtsies fit,
   Sails in and out the circle of thy ken.

TENNYSON ROCK.

MAJESTIC, awesome and inspiring mock,
   Sculptured by frost and sun and bitter brine!
   Has nature sympathy with men divine,
   To carve remembrance in colossal rock?
Circled by voices of the sea-god's flock,
   Deep calm is his, aloofness of the pine,—
   As when he waited his great Pilot's sign
   Ere he embarked from out earth's sheltered loch.

O seer and Englishman, our answering hearts
   Leapt at thy words of empire! Sure 'tis meet
   In "that true North" thy form should front the sea,
Where Howe, McDonald, Tupper played their parts
   At statecraft, gath'ring at Old England's feet
   Our Pleiad State,—one flag, one destiny.

OF BEAUTY.

THE convoluted wave, God's first sea-shell,
   Upgathers now the deep's great harmonies ;
   From the far blue an Alp-like cloud doth well,
   Baring its azured peaks to the heavenlies.
My spirit's outward bound, hath liberty !
   Earnest as rising flame its young love burns
   To catch the awesome gladness flowing free
   O'er earth and sky as Beauty's face upturns.

O naught is great without thy effluence !
   In curving billow's culminating sweep,
   In mountain heights, the strength of grace is seen.
Essence divine, of God-like competence,—
   Reposeful in the heart of things as sleep !
   Robed in the purple, sceptred, throned a queen !

THE UNDERTOW.

[B. B. D.]

O'er all the shining levels of the beach
   The tide outpours its hissing, foaming brine,
   While with the primal surge the winds combine
   To press the eager waves to utmost reach.
See yon brave billow, rising from the pleach
   Of seething waters, with a might divine,
   Its sinews wrought in beauty's flowing line,
   Leap forward now to make the age-sought breach !

Lo, as the cresting plume is seen aloft,
   The footing of its strength on sudden slips
   And all is whelmed in thunderous recoils !
Ah, tragedy of lusty life ! How oft
   Some high emprise a soul divinely grips,
   But as it crests fate's undertow despoils !

GLOOSCAP.

Dim name, yet grand, that ever winks serene
   In the red fagot's light, and like a ghost
   Hovers above these raucous tides, this coast,
   Wreathing weird webs of arrowy salts and keen !
Under the black blue night's unrollëd screen
   The loon is calling to the fiery host,
   And yet no answer comes to keep thy boast,—
   Far years their mellow thunders roll between.

Divinest of the red man's race and name,
   Fulness of Hiawatha's dawning day,
   Giver of laws, priest, prophet, all confest !
Thou'lt come again, appeased thy wrath and shame,
   Thy speed in all thy limbs, up yonder Bay
   In white canoe from out the naked west.

Oft did thy spell enthrall me, spite the cost !
   Thou brought'st a charmed and fadeless holiday—
   Stories and songs and Indian epic lay—
   Whene'er thy eager step the threshold crost.
Imagination all its plumes uptost
   To follow where thy spirit led the way !—
   (The sense that thou saw'st God when thou didst
      pray
   I never through the dimming years have lost.)

Fair Minas' shores thy step did gladden, too !
   Thou charm'dst great Glooscap from the unlet-
      tered past,
   And told'st his story to the listener nigh'st ;
Ay, lover of song, of learnëd lore and vast,
   Thou lov'dst the Indian with a love so true,
   In his sweet tongue thou gavest him the Christ.

33

THE TIRELESS SEA.

AGE after age the tireless sea doth fling
    Its serried waves against this frowning rock,
    (Whose base has known a thousand years of shock,)
    And shouts its purpose to its floor to bring.
High up and landward now the ravens wing,
    On trees sure-rooted inland nests the hawk ;
    Instinct of doom ! for here swift ships shall dock,
    And give of east and west, and commerce sing.

Warriors of truth, unwearied host of God,
    Who, like the deep, march to the signs of heaven,
    "Thus saith the Lord" your cry, count not the
        years !
Grey superstition's crumbling front shall nod
    Beneath the iteration of your steven,
    And God's sweet love flood all the place of tears.

THE VEILED PRESENCE.

An ashen grey touched faint my night-dark room,
   I flung my window wide to the whispering lawn—
   Great God! I saw Thy mighty globe from gloom
   Roll with its sleeping millions to the dawn.
No tremor spoke its motion swift and vast,
   In hush it swept the awful curve adown,
   The shadow that its rushing speed did cast
   Concealed the Father's hand, the Kingly crown.

Into the deeps an age has passed since then,
   Yet evermore for me, more humble grown,
   The vision of His awesome presence veiled,
Burns in the flying spheres, still all unknown,
   In nature's mist-immantled seas unsailed,
   And in the deeper shadowed hearts of men.

RESISTLESS FATE.

RESISTLESS fate and iron destiny
    Are writ upon the tide—its branded mark.
    It comes and goes heedless of wind or bark,
    Nature's untamed and tameless energy.
So rolls the cycle of eternity,—
    Days, months, and years—faint shadows on the arc
    Within our human ken—rush from the dark
    And speed return as God's own mystery.

I on this tide-beat shore, and clutching time,
    Marvel of what account my selfhood's will,—
    'Gainst timeless might time's impotence is laid!
And through my inmost soul, as at the prime,
    A voice from out the awesome vast doth thrill:
    "O man, thou art in God's own image made!"

Exquisite thing soft cradled by the tide,
    Sprung not from lathe or wheel or human wit,
    Wonder of whorls which touch the infinite,—
    Shallop that waits a brave undine's white bride !
Within, the smooth and sheeny walls are dyed
    With the pure pink of autumn dawns alit ;
    Without, with stories of the deep o'er-writ,—
    How fairy slight the thunderous seas to ride !

The massy tides gride over reef and ledge,
    And sudden waves from fell Euroclydon
    Dash to swift death the sailor in the Bay ;
But this, all lipt with pearl, and on the edge
    Of doom—the fingers of a babe might slay—
    Sleeps in the stressful surge at Blomidon.

TO EMELINE.

In white-spruce bower, with outlook on the sea,
  Kingcups and daisies dancing down the slope,
  And broad-winged ships, world-messengers of hope,
  Furling their plumes or lifting them all free
To catch the skyey airs—here 'tis that we
  Oft watch the fringes of the tide, where ope
  The swinging doors through which all blind-fold
      grope
  The muffled waves of shoreless mystery.

The touch of two vast worlds is on us now.
  Our spirits hear the ebb and flow unseen
  Of swift commingling tides of far and near,—
The low sweet murmur of the early vow,
  Commerce of life's strange sea, on wing between,
  And folding plumes arrived the heavenly pier.

THE CIRRUS CLOUD.

Thou hast the secret of the fiery dew,
　　Variety and number infinite
　　Are vestured in thy wavy flakes of white,—
　　Of distance and of space thou hast the clue.
Aloof from vapory clouds that fume and spue,
　　Lifting thyself victorious in fight
　　Into the far repose of zonëd light,
　　Thou strivest to attain nirvâna-blue.

Mottled, or plumed, or ribbed, or ripple-barred,
　　Encamped upon the unfenced fields of space,
　　Unsullied are thy tents cool-washed in air;
And when morn's bugle blows, or sky's new-starred,
　　Thy cohorts wait day's coming, parting face,
　　Like flocks of rosy angels drifting there.

DAY AND NIGHT.

And so the strife goes on from age to age,
   In ceaseless round of victory and defeat :
   Young Day comes forth, sun-clad, with shining feet,
   In beauteous pomp, and throws his battle-gage.
Grim ancient Night, distraught and blind with rage,
   Twanging her dreadful bow, flies in retreat,
   Wrapt round with raven darkness as a sheet,
   Till from the east she may the duel wage.

So Night, pursuing wounded Day, takes breath
   To find his blood-stained mantle in the west,
   And dusks it o'er with plumëd shafts of death.
Secure beneath the horizon's verge, in wrath
   He wings a Parthian arrow back his path,
   And dyes with crimson Ethiop's jeweled vest.

UNDER THE BEECHES.

THE sibyl's speech breaks from these leafen lips,
    Moved by soft airs from shadowy spaces blown :
    " We rear these giant boles amid eclipse,
    We workmen die, the work abides alone."
The day has met the night beneath the sky,
    And the hot earth put off its robe of flame ;
    Sweet peace and rest come with the night-bird's cry,
    Sweet rest and peace the herald stars proclaim.

'Tis very heaven to taste the wells of sleep,
    The founts of supersensuous repose !—
    The sibyl's rune still murmurs on the breeze,
The purple night falls thick about the trees,
    And blessed stars, like lilies white and rose,
    Burst into bloom on heaven's far azure deep.

THE NIGHTINGALE.

O seraph bird who on God's altar-stairs
   Dost ring, in showers of silver peals, thy bells
   Of song that ceaseless flows like dropping-wells,
   And sprinkles all the dusk with holy prayers!
O welkin glad, shot through and through with song,
   As upward springs the spirit tipt with flame!
   'Tis not to Itys dead nor Dian's shame
   These joy-pangs, with their hint of tears, belong.

The life which pulses in the bursting year
   A thousand choirs hymn on the sunlit globe:
   But, lest the living flame to ashes turn,
Thou, in the voiceless night, O priestly seer,
   Interpreter of nature, tak'st thy robe,
   And fill'st with vocal fire the sacred urn.

THE LOON.

'NEATH northern skies thou hid'st thy punctual nest
   By crystal waters in their lonely play,
   Meeting the challenge with which instant day
   And night thy chariness and courage test.
Half bird, half spirit !—O elusive quest
   That thinks thy dappled mould but common clay !
   Thou wak'st with demon laughter Ha Ha Bay,
   Art soul of solitariness, unblest.

Flash of pure wildness on dusk Saguenay,
   Awareness of wild nature's subtle breast,
   Freight and athrill with weirdsome life, yet gay,
Thou cleav'st the deluge dense, a wingëd jest !—
   That rallying mock and jeer's an impish mark—
   The echo of thy flout of Noah's ark !

HEPATICAS.

A SHINING troop of cherubs just alit
    From the low-bending skies,—child faces sweet,
    Upturned and open to our human greet,—
    Fresh from the gladsome fount of life emit!
Heralds of spring, forewinging, as ye flit,
    The garland seasons with their sheaves of wheat,
    And to all listening ears Christ's words repeat:
    " Man shall not live by bread alone, 'tis writ " !

Evangelists fair of the new-made year,
    This news from God, forgot, blow everywhere,
    And fill the hollow sky, the haunting air;
Till from His loving mouth, as sphere to sphere,
    Man knows the beautiful, the good, the true,
    Divinest manna dipt in heavenly dew!

IN THE MAYFLOWER COPSE.

WITH gladsome note the robin debonair
    Heralds bright May.   Pale sky and earth-stained
        snow
    Warm at the touch of south winds as they blow
    Their wafts of life through winter's lingering air.
Hid, like some laughing child, shy Mayflower fair,
    Beneath the leafy shield, with face aglow,
    Thy pearly self the coy spring's first tableau,
    Come to the day and yield thy fragrance rare !

Ah me ! while thrushes pipe and plumy winds
    Fan northward all their balmy fervors sweet,
    And groves are misty with the reddening bud,
A gentle spirit from the past unbinds
    The peace of Lethe, and with quickening beat
    Stirs to divine unrest my fevered blood.

JUNE.

Now weave the winds to music of June's lyre
    Their bowers of cloud whence odorous blooms are
        flung
    Far down the dells and cedarn vales among,—
    See, lowly plains, sky-touched, to heaven aspire !
Now flash the golden robin's plumes with fire,
    The bobolink is bubbling o'er with song,
    And leafy trees, Æolian harps new-strung,
    Murmur far notes blown from some starry choir.

My heart thrills like the wilding sap to flowers,
    And leaps as a swoln brook in summer rain
    Past meadows green to the great sea untold.
O month divine, all fresh with falling showers,
    Waft, waft from open heaven thy balm for pain,
    Life and sweet Earth are young, God grows not
        old !

AN INLAND SPRUCE.

PEASANT of northern forests, humble tree,
   Kirtled and frocked in all-year homespun green,
   And lacking not among thy kind the mien
   Of such as bear the white sails gallantly !
Magician thou ! Thy full-breathed symphony
   Of spacious dream dissolves the walls between
   Me now and nature's organ-voicëd queen,
   The multitudinous ongoing sea !

The sheeny garb from thy tall shoulders hung,
   Making thy spiry form like vase antique
   For resinous balms of frankincense and myrrh,
And round the bearded skirts the drowsy purr
   Of life, and murmurings of thy sea-harp strung,—
   Touch thee to kinship fine with Celt and Greek.

THE GHOST FLOWER.

LIKE Israel's seer I come from out the earth
   Confronting with the question air and sky,
    Why dost thou bring me up? White ghost am I
   Of that which was God's beauty at its birth.
In eld the sun kissed me to ruby red,
   I held my chalice up to heaven's full view,
   The wistful stars dropt down their golden dew,
   And skyey balms exhaled about my bed.
Alas, I loved the darkness, not the light!
   The deadly shadows, not the bending blue,
   Spoke to my trancëd heart, made false seem true,
And drowned my spirit in the deeps of night.
   O Painter of the flowers, O God most sweet,
   Dost say my spirit for the light is meet?

ANNAPOLIS BASIN.

THE full-fed crystal streams from east and west
    And south, thy rich-wrought cup filled to the brim,
    Till where the northern star soft gilds the rim,
    Thy waters, called, o'erbroke at love's behest.
O to have seen thy cataract's white breast,
    Rifted with ruth through the lone centuries dim,
    For toiling Fundy's wooing tide—for him
    To blend thy sylvan calm with world unrest !
Far floods thy bridal brought, fair lake, brave sea !
    And late, the wingëd ships—Champlain, De Monts,
    With Poutrincourt, and sequent games of war.
Thy marge, now crowned with peaceful husbandry,
    And set with England's rose where bloomed *fleur
        d'or,*
    Still croons all day love's wedded tidal song.

IN AUTUMN'S DREAMY EAR.

In autumn's dreamy ear, as suns go by
   Whose yellow beams are dulled with languorous
      motes,
   The deep vibrations of the cosmic notes
   Are as the voice of those that prophesy.
Her spirit kindles, and her filmy eye!
   In haste the fluttering robe, whose glory floats
   In pictured folds, her eager soul devotes—
   Lo, she with her winged harper sweeps the sky!

Splendors of blossomed time, like poppies red,
   Distil dull slumbers o'er the engagéd soul
   And thrall with sensuous pomp its azured dower;
'Till, roused by vibrant touch from the unseen Power,
   The spirit keen, freed from the painted dead,
   On wings mounts up to reach its living Goal.

VICTOR IS HE!

VICTOR is he whose tremulous soul the notes
    Of starry spaces hears, their far appeal,
    And cries "Amen!" and sets thereto the seal
    With which winged aspiration life devotes!
That seal rays golden flame, and bright connotes
    The transmutation through the spirit's zeal
    Of earthly passions to the high anneal
    That rings the harmony that heavenward floats.

While other triremes vain withstood the guile,
    The lyric prow of Orpheus easeful past
    In gladsome scorn's disdain the Sirens' Isle;
And proud Calliope o'er each black mast
    Whispered her thrilling taunt in ears of pain:
    "I taught my Thracian boy a heavenlier strain!"

McMASTER UNIVERSITY.

As some grey captain of a merchantship,
    Whose prosperous voyage o'er the watery strife
    Has large concern for all, knows that his wife
    Waits his home-coming up the horizon's dip
With holier heart than crowds that throng the slip,
    So He well knew, thou—flower-elect of life !
    Chosen from out a clamor of voices rife—
    Waitedst his voyage o'er with prayerful lip.

Fair Bride, forget him not through circling years !
    But with a Christ-like love, deep as unfeigned
    Surpassing that of commerce or of state,
With holy hands thy dower devote with tears
    Of gratitude and loyal heart unstained ;
    Thy sacred vow perform with soul elate.

CONDUCT.

Nay, Arnold, not "three-fourths" but all "of life"!
   The ethic spirit that makes conduct so,
   Slays all mythologies and witchcrafts, lo,
   False sciences as well, with ruthless knife,
Lest intercourse of human souls be rife
   With demi-gods and unclean things below,
   And work corruption at the founts that flow,
   From hearts of fellowmen in loving strife.

That spirit more than science is the hope
   Of man's uplifting, and doth knowledge make
   Servant of individual, social worth.
Not truth for truth's own sake, as tense we cope
   With life, but rather truth for love's own sake
   Calls forth heaven's plaudit round the girdled earth.

INTERNATIONAL ARBITRATION.

Boom, boom, ye mellow joy-bells, like the sea!
  Peace, peace on earth, good-will! (and all hell
      gapes!)—
  Yet immemorial sadness ever drapes
  The upward way of far humanity:
All prone through dark and strait Gethsemane
  Thou cam'st in blood, a cluster of trod grapes!—
  O bruisèd race, whose wail so surgeful shapes
  Melodious sorrow's awful threnody!

Late, late, love's Areopagus unfurled
  Right-reason's sun-glad banner from the height,
  While rage the Furies in their cave beneath!
Hush, hush, it is the daybreak of the world!
  Man's warring sky is passing out of night,
  And stark black demons flit with sword in sheath.

THE HOUSE OF GOD.

[G. A. G.]

No finished castle is the house of God.
   The mind of Christ, supremest Architect,
   Man's puny apprehension doth correct
   From age to age, and turns afresh the sod.
The vast historic temple now is trod
   'Neath loftier roof and heavenlier aspéct;
   New light, new need, revealed, each ripe defect
   Goes down beneath man's feet diviner shod.

Alas, humanity no more can grasp
   Of thought of the divine Artificer,
   Than holds of ocean crinkled shell on beach !
Yet His unfolding plan in vital clasp
   Possess, O human soul, amid the stir
   Of speeding worlds Love's flying-goal to reach !

BEN NACHMANI.

"O THE brightness, clearness, beauty of heaven !
  Seer Ben Nachmani," Rabbi Levi said,
    "Of the Hagada Master thou of seven,
    Would that I knew whence Light, its fountain-
        head ?"
The Master whispered in the Rabbi's ear :
    "The Holy One, blessëd be He, in white
    Himself doth robe, and then the whole world clear
    In beauty glows with His majestic light."
"Sayest thou so ? That's word for word the psalm :
    'The light Thy garment is which Thou dost wear.'
    Thou tell'st it here a secret 'neath the palm,
    O Master thou of seven with whitened hair !"

And softer fell the Master's whispered word :
"I heard it thus; O Rabbi, hast thou heard?"

RENEWAL.

'IN the old days Vannucci, color-dowered,
   Lit up young eyes with vision large and pure,
   That gathered in its iris-glow the lure
   Of sea and sky, and beauty earth-embowered;
And Rafael Santi on the master showered
   The rich-hued passion of his soul, secure
   In art that should for evermore endure,—
   But as he wrought his vision was defloured.
For sake of art divine a seer bright-stoled,
   Whose eyes had drunk the steadfast splendors true
   Of sacred gems, this precious secret told:
   " Oft sight of these doth color-sense renew ! "

Ah thus, true soul assoiled of life, thou ey'st,
Mid thy enduring work, the quickening Christ !

THE CHRIST.

THE noonday Truth
  In its sevenfold beam,
    Is the Christ, sandal-shod ;
  Yea, the Truth in warm gleam
Of color and shine,
Both of age and of youth,
  As on life's plains and wolds
  His soul's prism unfolds
    The white thought of God,
In human passion divine.

REVELATION.

As rising waves, rich jeweled by the sun,
  In movement link their brilliants each to each,
  And flash their glories in one crest of light,
E'en so, unveiling, the Eternal One
  Did shew Himself by signs and glimmering speech,
  Then flashed in Christ His love-lit glory bright.

LIGHT AT EVENTIDE.

THROUGH skies of molten gold and green the sun
    Floats with its cloud-wake o'er the glowing rim
    Of closing day; the same horizon brim
Glows green and gold with a glad day begun.
So closes life's full day, its guerdon won,
    To those whose trustful souls are joined to Him—
    The world's great Light—whose hand the splen-
        dors limn
At once of breaking day and day that's done.

BEN SHALOM.

BEN SHALOM read one night from out a roll:
"Vessel of honor, consecrate ('O soul!')
Prepared for every worthy work, and meet
For the Master's use!"   And finger on scroll,
He prayed aloud: "Make me his silvern bowl!"
Lo!   Emeth at his side, God's angel fleet:
"Yea, in His mansion here; and when unfold
The everlasting doors, chalice of gold
Brimming with His great love—heaven's vintage
        sweet!"

E   59

BANISHMENT.

As tiptoe dawn extinguished all the stars,
There lay on a fevered flower the cooling dew ;
Full soon the scornful sun, with white heat glare,
Forever bade the offending thing from view ;
But as day closed, it outshone flaming Mars,
Or wheeling splendors of the Northern Bear.

NOW ARE THE BRIDALS OF THE LEAFY WOOD.

Now are the bridals of the leafy wood,
   O'er dusky brooks the golden sunbars fall,
   Birds fan the moonbeams in the balmy dark—
Look me ! the banners of the holy rood
   Shake in the battle's roar ; sweet duty's call
   Wings all my spirit like a soaring lark.

MAY'S FAIRY TALE.

UNDER the yellow chestnut tree
The children played right merrily.

From leafy gold came pattering down
The prickly burs with nuts of brown.

"I do believe," said bright-eyed May,
"We're pelted by some startled fay!

For fairies love no tree so well
As chestnut broad in which to dwell."

"Tell us a fairy tale," they said,
"A fairy tale," they eager pled,

" About the fairies of to-day ! "
And circled round the wise-eyed May.

With air of one who tells new truth,
The gentle May, with touch of ruth,

This tale of Elfland sweetly told,
While all stood deep in autumn's gold :

" Long, long ago the fairies found
Their homes in flowers on the ground.

The buttercups were full of them,
And pansies sparkled like a gem.

But fields by men were often mown,
The flowers were plucked as soon as grown.

Thus without tents to shed cold dews,
The pixies lost their brilliant hues.

Their kirtles green and mantles gold
Were crushed and torn and smeared with mould.

(You should have seen Mab's ermine cape,
Draggled in muck till black as crape !)

At last, his gossamer hammocks gone,
Their daylight king, bright Oberon,

(Who could not find two crimson heads
Of clover strung with spider-webs)

And Mab, the moonlight queen of elves
Took solemn counsel with themselves.

'Twas in the early summer days
They met at twilight all the fays,

Under a grove with fronded plumes,
Whose trees were white with spikes of blooms.

With elfin lance of wild-bee sting
Stood Oberon, at the outer ring.

His knights each wore upon his breast
A firefly lamp in beetle's vest.

MAY'S FAIRY TALE.

With glow-worm crown of greenish light,
Sitting her fairy palfrey white,

The queen, by wave of saffron brand,
Hushed into silence fairyland.

Then with her sandaled foot she pricked
Her wasp-sting spur (and palfrey kicked!)—

Her moonbeam bridle firm in grip,
She plied the silken milkweed whip,

And rode straight up the waiting tree,
And out each branch its blooms to see.

When Mab (her own and palfrey's wings
Of gauzy blue outspread) the rings

Of wistful pixies leapt into,
Sitting erect her horse so true,

In silvery laughter broke each fay,
Like silvery tinkling brook in May.

Waving her saffron brand, she said :
' Fairies ! your future home and bed !'

And pointed up the flower-lit tree,—
Thither they swarmed as swarms the bee !

In turn each bole and fronded roof
Was trod by Elf-queen palfrey's hoof,

Till fays who bore the flame-wood lamp,
Swung in their peaceful airy camp.

That was a chestnut grove they found !
And as the sunny spring comes round,

Queen Mab, when shines the silver moon,
And elfin bugles blow in tune,

Still rides high up each chestnut tree,
That fays may know where safe they'll be,

And golden-belted Oberon
Swing in his hammock like a Don,—

For palfrey prints his tiny shoe
On every branch that's wet with dew.

My story's told, now for our play!"
"And is the story true, O May?"

With air of one who knows the truth,
The sweet-eyed May, tall for her youth,

The overhanging branch down drew,
And shewed the prints of palfrey's shoe—

And laughing said: "Now you all see
Why it is called *Horse*-Chestnut tree."

MY ROBIN.

[E. B. D.]

At the very dawn of day,
  My robin from the hill flies down,
And from the fence across the way,
  With black cap on his handsome head,
  And slatish cloak and vest of red,
  He calls me from my easeful bed:
    Dear *up*, dear *up*, dear !
    Cheer up, cheer up, cheer !

Constant as the coming morn,
  He leaves his green fir copse to see
If I will greet his breezy horn,
  And share his joy that day is here

MY ROBIN.

To shimmer the sea, the fog to clear,
And yellow the corn of the hasting year :
   Dear *up*, dear *up*, dear !
   Cheer up, cheer up, cheer !

Ah robin, so debonair,
  So glad of the darkness gone away,
So heedful of this heart of care,
  Sweet to me is your roundelay,
  Born of a spirit so tender, so gay,—
  Let me join you in duet for aye !
   Dear up, dear up, dear !
   Cheer up, cheer up, cheer !

ELISSA.

I HOLD my secret fast!
  Sunset I watch, and dawn,
Wait the white moonbeam cast,
  The pall of night down-drawn.
Then in the ebon dark
  I whisper to myself,
While every sense doth hark
  Lest blade, or leaf, or elf,
Should catch the trembling word,
  And all the listening air
Be to its utmost stirred,
  The giddy world aware!

The willow heedful is,
  And the titmouse peers at me,

The kingcups nod and quiz
   With an air of mystery;
But no one knows at all—
   I hold my secret fast!
The wizard loon may call
   Till night be overpast,
Troops of bright eyes may smile,
   The people look me o'er,
The parson turn the stile,
   Friends tarry at the door!

I hold my secret fast!
   Sunset I watch, and dawn,
See the blue heavens o'ercast,
   The pail of night down-drawn;
And then in raven dark
   I whisper to myself,—
My whitest soul ahark
   Lest blade, or leaf, or elf,
Should hear the trembling word,
   And all the listening air
Be to its farthest stirred,
   The rolling world aware

THE HUMMING-BIRD.

Thought-sudden presence
  Out of blank air—
  Humming of wings!
Here—a whisk and a flash!
  Sipping red balm there—
  And the silence sings.

Thy will works its end
  In freedom complete,—
  Deed flashing in sheen;
Forward or backward
  As easeful, as fleet,
  As a spirit unseen.

71

THE HUMMING-BIRD.

Plumed gem all athrob,
   Thy ruby throat burns
   As from the hot kiss
Of a heaven-smit soul
   As it panteth and yearns,
   In its rapture of bliss!

Thing of beauty, of life,
   Bright wink of a day
   When we'll be what we are—
Freed of this garment's hem!
O soul, get thy wings,
   Find the red balm for aye,
   (Life of earth and of star!)
Flash with love, a live gem!

THE HEPATICA.

HAIL, first of the spring,
Pearly sky-tinted thing
    Touched with pencil of Him
Who rollest the year!
    Lo, thy aureole rim
    No painter may limn—
Vision thou hast, and no fear!

Fair child of the light,
What fixes thy sight?
    Wide-open thy roll
From the seal of the clod,
    And thy heaven-writ scroll
    Glows, beautiful soul,
With the shining of God!

THE HEPATICA.

Thou look'st into heaven
As surely as Stephen,
　So steadfast thy will is !
And from earth's inglenook
　Seest Christ of the lilies
　And daffadowndillies,
And catchest His look.

And a portion is mine,
Rapt gazer divine,
　From thy countenance given—
Angel bliss in thy face !
　I've looked into heaven
　As surely as Stephen,
From out of my place !

THE WHITE ROSE.

(AT ——'S GRAVE.)

Rose pendent in calm of the sun,
  (A type of my holiest thought)
Fair substance and emblem in one,—
  Sweet rose—sweet soul without spot !
Sweetness of beauty of God
Both over and under the sod.

Each moulded in earth's cloud and shine,
  White fulness of being complete,
Love's rose of beauty divine !
  Thy past, but evolvings sweet,
Now, moment of essence for aye,
Thy future, eternity's day !

F

THE WHITE ROSE.

O rose in the mirror of time—
   Calm image from under the sod—
O form of eternal prime,
   All-peaceful beauty of God,—
Fulness of seventy times seven,
Made without hands, in the heaven !

What though thy time-garment fade
   And vanish from out of my sight,
Thy beauty shall never know shade
   With the Chief of the sons of light—
Redeemed from under the sod,
Ravishing beauty of God !

THE WAR HERCULES.

UNDER Mount Œta
   The blue Artemisium,
Flanked about with huge crags,
   Stilled its wild winter drum,—
The sun turned aside,
   The sea nestled in calm,
   Zeus's wisdom of calm,—
Rude Hercules died!

A wine-glass of azure
   From the breast of the bay,
Caught up by the sun,
Smiled on by the sun,—
   Hope's halcyon ray!

THE WAR HERCULES.

Kiss of love for a bride,
   Kiss of peace and of calm,
   Zeus's wisdom of calm,—
Wild Hercules died!

A nest and a home
   On the wintry sea,
On the blue Artemise,
   In the rough country,
Heaven set in the azure tide!
   The sea nestled in calm,
   Zeus's wisdom of calm,—
Fierce Hercules died!

O halcyon of rest,
   Sweet azure of peace,
Brood thy sky-tinted eggs,
   Fill the world with increase—
On the sea's bosom ride!
   Now it nestles to calm,
   Zeus's wisdom of calm,—
Mad Hercules died!

January, 1896.

IN THE COOL OF THE DAY.

I.

To him that hears the calling in the calm,
   And, naked, feeds his soul at Wisdom's lip,
Bird, grove, and brook—God's voice in silver psalm—
   Are like a secret honeycomb adrip.

II.

Remote in thought from every living thing,
   Silent the sage without his threshold sate,
Pondering the mysteries of Gyges' ring,
   Dreaming of timeless years and iron fate.

79

The whirr of sudden wings his ear awoke,—
    A lark rose free in its grey singing robe.
"O miracle of life," in speech he broke,
    "A bird is greater than the solid globe !"

III.

But yesterday I saw a hillside grove
    Whose trunks were clad with lichens grey as frost ;
At night a storm of rain and wind fierce drove,—
    Each bole to-day in living green's embossed !

And so, I said, the clinging lives which make
    Yearful and spectral those who yield them ruth,
Shall, when o'er these the night in storm doth break,
    Wreathe them in freshness of immortal youth.

IV.

Adown the steep cliff's face I saw unurn
    Its waters full, a crystal brook to-day ;
The silvery bubbles coursed each scar by turn,
    Safe as on a full-fed meadow stream in May.

I thought of that sweet Scripture Satan used
    To tempt the Christ, and knew it true *they* bear
In woven hands our souls, else deadly bruised,
    By hell thrust down some precipice's stair.

v.

Still at the breeze of day doth nature's God
    Forth in earth's paradisal bowers walk,
And of soul-freedom, Love's restoring rod,
    And angel guardianship, He deigns to talk.

BEAUTY.

I.

"HAD I two loaves of bread—ay, ay!
One would I sell and hyacinths buy
To feed my soul."—"Or let me die!"

Beauty, dew-sweet, of heavenly birth,
Thy flower is writ of grief, not mirth,
Thy rainbow's footed on the earth.

Rainbows and hyacinths!   O seers,
Your voices call across the years:
"The bread of Beauty's wet with tears!

II.

The living words from Beauty's mien,
Than blade by swordsman swung more keen,
Spirit and soul divide between :

" Pure as the sapphire-blue from blame,
Humble as glad, of holiest aim—
Love's seven-fold beam a flashing flame !"

III.

It yearns me sore, so near, so far !
My heart moans like the harbor-bar,
For coming of the morning star.

Buy hyacinths—a goodly share !
Ascend, O soul, love's iris-stair,
The bridegroom waiteth for thee there !

THE DRAGONFLY.

I.

WINGED wonder of motion
In splendor of sheen,
Cruising the shining blue
Waters all day,
Smit with hunger of heart
And seized of a quest
Which nor beauty of flower
Nor promise of rest
Has charm to appease
Or slacken or stay,—
   What is it you seek,
   Unopen, unseen?

II.

Are you blind to the sight
Of the heavens of blue,
Or the wind-fretted clouds
On their white, airy wings,
Or the emerald grass
That velvets the lawn,
Or glory of meadows
Aflame like the dawn?
  Are you deaf to the note
  In the woodland that rings
  With the song of the whitethroat,
  As crystal as dew?

III.

Winged wonder of motion
In splendor of sheen,
Stay, stay a brief moment
Thy hither and thither
Quick-beating wings,

85

Thy flashes of flight ;
And tell me thy heart,
Is it sad, is it light,

Is it pulsing with fears
Which scorch it and wither,
   Or joys that up-well
   In a girdle of green ?

IV.

" O breather of words
And poet of life,
I tremble with joy,
I flutter with fear !
Ages it seemeth,
Yet only to-day
Into this world of
Gold sunbeams at play,
I came from the deeps.
   O crystalline sphere !
   O beauteous light !
   O glory of life !

v.

"On the watery floor
Of this sibilant lake,
I lived in the twilight dim.
'There's a world of Day,'
Some pled, 'a world
Of ether and wings athrob
Close over our head.'
'It's a dream, it's a whim,
A whisper of reeds,' they said,—
    And anon the waters would sob.
And ever the going
Went on to the dead
Without the glint of a ray,
    And the watchers watched
    In their vanishing wake.

VI.

"The passing
Passed for aye,
And the waiting

Waited in vain!
Some power seemed to enfold
The tremulous waters around,
Yet never in heat
Nor in shrivelling cold,
Nor darkness deep or grey,—
Came token of sound or touch,—
A clear unquestioned 'Yea!'
   And the scoffers scoffed,
   In swelling refrain,
   'Let us eat and drink,
   For to-morrow we die.'

VII.

"But, O, in a trance of bliss,
With gauzy wings I awoke!
An ecstasy bore me away
O'er field and meadow and plain.
   I thought not of recent pain,
   But revelled, as splendors broke
   From sun and cloud and air,
   In the eye of golden Day.

VIII.

" I'm yearning to break
To my fellows below
The secret of ages hoar ;
In the quick-flashing light
I dart up and down,
Forth and back, everywhere,
But the waters are sealed
Like a pavement of glass,—
Sealed that I may not pass.
    O for waters of air !
    Or the wing of an eagle's might
    To cleave a pathway below !"

IX.

And the Dragonfly in splendor
Cruises ever o'er the lake,
Holding in his heart a secret
Which in vain he seeks to break.

DEATHLESS.

I.

THE coy soul of man,
Moving through its time-span,
Unheeding of wings,
Tastes the death of all things—
Of the flower and weed
And the faint-voiced reed.

II.

The fair seasons roll
    For you and for me.
The inhabiting soul
    Of the flower and tree,

With the day of each
   Born to be and to die,—
No eternity-speech,
   No eternity-cry
That pierces above,
   Nor infinite thrill
At the touch of Love,
   Or the voice of His will—
From His fingers begot,—
God-breathed it is not !

III.

'Twas a shy fair one,
   Like a beam of light   '
From the clouded sun,
   That rose to the sight
Of the eye of emotion
   In the soul of the Greek,
And eternized the form ;
   And vision, devotion,
Ever fixt on the norm,—

Type of beauty of flower,
Of grove and of bower,
Deathless, unique!

IV.

Not from pole unto pole
Is man's hunger of soul,
But eternity's set
As a deathless fret
In the heart of man
As it beats the earth-span,—
Beating not from the sod,
But an ongoing of God!
And it listens for Him
Over Time's flying rim,
And it sips, or it stings,
A life from all things—
From the flower and the weed
And the faint-voiced reed.

A DREAM.

I DREAMED the Lord of Life was dead.
　Tremulous awe fell on the earth,
Virtue had gone from out all things,
　The sun and rain were nothing worth.

Rude power seized the painted woods
　And hurled their glory down the steep,
The landscape wrapt in cerements
　And left in death's eternal sleep.

Nor bloom nor odor met the sense,
　Nor wind-chant of the foliaged tree,
Nor grove of singing birds, nor psalm
　Borne from the ever-voiceful sea.

93

A DREAM.

Color had fled the air and sky,
　　A stony stillness held the earth,
Virtue had gone from out all things,
　　Man's ebbing life was nothing worth.

And as I wept within my dream
　　And knew my pulse of being slowed,
I sudden was aware of change—
　　A flush on pallid nature showed!

Lo, heralds of the arriving year!
　　The bugled flock beclangs the blue,
The hyla pipes by willowed run,
　　The flashing swallow skims the dew.

Up from the rampike's ghastly arms
　　The gold-shaft high-hole's challenge floats,
While greening hill and valley laugh
　　And shore breaks out in pæan notes.

And in my dream I leapt for joy—
　　"'Twas but an awful dream," I said,

A DREAM.

"The Lord of Life, for evermore
  He lives—'twas once for all He bled!"

And waked from sleep by beating heart,
  I heard the first red robin sing,
And knew that once again had come
  Fresh from the life of God the spring.

NATURE.

THE large, far intent
  Of the Kingly One
  Is only begun
In rearing the tent;
  To nurture a soul
  Is the shining goal.

Keen science speaketh
  A word clear and fair:
  "The carbon in air
The young oak seeketh
  In the greening years,
  Lo, a giant appears!

96

" Shelter and warmth, see !
    Here final cause
    Of nature's wise laws ;
And the breath of the tree
    Is life unto man
    And lengthens his span.'

But the Chemist who moves
    The atoms in dance,
    His all-seeing glance
By His working proves,—
    From far-off to nigher,
    Feeds life that is higher.

From blade to full ear,
    From acorn to beam,
    Unfoldings of dream,
Linkëd series of cheer,
    Evolvings of grace,
    Shadows bright of His face !

Sweet procession and slow,
    Every step of the way
    More precious each day,

NATURE.

Till the starlit airs blow,
    Wake emotion that sleeps,
    Stir the fount of the deeps.

O heaven's own fact
    Eternal, that beauty,
    As the sword on duty,
Hangs silent on act
    Of nature forever,—
    Soul and body together !

Nature, series divine
    Of act and of word
    From God's mouth seen or heard !
As thou bring'st bread and wine
    I hear thy deep tone,
    "O not these alone !"

All-divine unity !
    Writes the heaven-touched mind
    Responsive, once blind :
All-divine harmony !
    Emotion's attest
    In the glow of my breast.

"I AM."

I AM, and therefore these,
  Existence is by me,—
Flux of pendulous seas,
  The stable, free.

I am in blush of the rose,
  The shimmer of dawn ;
Am girdle Orion knows,
  The fount undrawn.

I am earth's potency,
  The chemic ray's, the rain's,
The reciprocity
  That loads the wains.

99

"*I AM.*"

I am, or the heavens fall!
  I dwell in my woven tent,
Am immanent in all,—
  Suprámanent!

I am the Life in life,
  Impact and verve of thought,
The reason's lens and knife,
  The ethic "ought."

I am of being the stress,
  I am the brooding Dove,
I am the blessing in "bless,"
  The Love in love.

I am the living thrill
  And fire of poet and seer,
The breath of man's goodwill,
  The Father near;

Am end of the way men grope,
  Core of the ceaseless strife,
I am man's bread of hope,
  Water of life.

"*I AM.*"

I am the root of faith,
   Substance of vision, too,
The spirit shadowed in wraith,
   Urim in dew.

I am the soul's white Sun,
   Love's slain, enthronëd Lamb,
I am the Holy One,
   I am I AM!

THE GLAD GOLDEN YEAR.

THE glad golden year
 Wheels slow in its coming.
Wild labor commotions
 And murmurings for bread
While besotted with beer
 Is the day's up-summing,—
Insurgent emotions
 To beauty stone-dead !

What help, do you say,
 For these sons of men ?
In God's image they're made—
 Cleanse their eyes to His light,
Tune their ears to His lay,
 Give His bread once again

Whose price the Christ paid,—
    Heaven's bread is their right!

Earth's means of achieving
    (Herds, field-food, and river,
Rain-cisterns in sky,
    And sunshine elysian)
Forever are weaving,
    And fain would deliver,
Web of God's beauty nigh—
    Sense-ravishing vision!

Sow bread in the field :
    Warm rain will transfigure
The humble grey furrow
    With a million pearl suns
On the lanceolate shield
    Of emerald and ligure,
And the moon o'er each burrow
    Of the low-buried ones
Turn silver the spear-tips
In the dusk, with her lips ;
    And when breezy morn's told,
    All ripples in gold.

With envious repining
  Or solace of delight—
As emotion is pure
  Or turbid with ill—
Man views the outshining
  From the heavenly height,
Feels the sweet picture's lure,
  Hears the bird-copse athrill,
Makes him lord, or does not,
Of the park, house, or cot.

Who holds the sure key
  To this largesse of treasure
Is a king among men,
  Though a workman in blue,—
Of a strain yet to be
  Who with God taketh pleasure
In the young earth again,
  And feeleth it new.
Slow speeds the glad year
Told by poet and seer,
  Yet I catch the far hum—
  It will come, it will come!

TETRAPLA.

LOVE.

THE blooming flowers, the galaxies of space,
    Lie pictured in a sheeny drop of even ;
And globed in one round word, on lips of grace,
    Shine out the best of earth and all of heaven.

SACRIFICE.

Green-haloed cup of the gods, cool from the deeps,
    Fountain of life, whence comes thy wave that
        blesses ?
" The burdened cloud attempts the mountain steeps,
    To perish 'mid the rugged wildernesses."

TETRAPLA.

LIBERTY.

Thou rugged Gaian of man's free behests,
   Belted and helmed 'neath God's red thunder-flails ;
World climes upon thy many-cloven crests,
   And ordered kingdoms in thy fertile vales !

BEAUTY.

The grace of strength the shaggy hills attest,
   And cresting billows in their power serene ;
Beauty was suckled at no weakling's breast,
   She sits the manëd lion like a queen.

FAIRY GLEN.

Hid in the virgin wilderness,
  The fretted Conway's Fairy Glen
This summer day reveals its charms
  For painter's brush or poet's pen.

The air is flecked with night and day,
  The ground is tiger-dusk and -gold,
The rocks and trees, empearled in haze,
  A soft and far enchantment hold.

The place is peopled with shy winds
  Whose fitful plumes waft dewy balm
From all the wildwood, and let fall
  An incommunicable calm.

H   107

FAIRY GLEN.

Through cleft rocks green with spray-wet moss,
   Deep in the sweet wood's golden glooms,
The amber waters pulsing go,
   With foam like creamy lily blooms.

Shuttles of shadow and of light
   In-gleam and -gloom the watery woof
As rolls the endless stream away
   Beneath the wind-swayed leafy roof.

(So life's swift shuttles dart and play,
   As ceaseless speeds its flashing loom ;
Our day is woven of sun and cloud,
   A figured web of gold and gloom.)

God's arbor, this enchanted Glen !
   The air is sentient with His name ;
Put off thy shoes from off thy feet,
   The trees are bursting into flame !

IN CITY STREETS.

THE city's ways were crowded thick,—
  I bent my steps athrough its mass
Of men and women, stone and brick,
  Its whirring wheels and piping brass.

And all day long, with hurrying feet,
  I trod the surging marts of trade ;
Yet in the rush and roar of street
  A calm within my breast was made.

For visions came of fair things wrought
  By beauty's witching hand and grace
Upon my spirit when I caught
  Life's spring-time image of her face :—

Blue violets in mossy bed,
 Flashing with jewels on their breast ;
The sky-stained eggs of robin red
 Laid in her lined adobe nest ;

The shy lone brook, crept soft upon
 Lest I should fright its brattling play :
The woods ahark for something gone,
 Or whispering of elf and fay ;

The silver lake with lilies in bloom,
 Their cups half-full of heaven's gold,
The circling shore all prankt with plume
 Of ferns, whose fronds the waters told ;

And up the hill the whitethroat's song—
 A crystal bell that shakes the dew !
While floats in dream the cloud along,
 And veils the palpitating blue ;

The musical and dream-like rain
 Falling on roof o'er fragrant hay ;
The blood-red spear, unflushed of pain,
 Of sunbeam thrust 'tween battens grey ;

And in a trice, the sculptured shore
   Where halcyon tides with wonder-wings
Redden their plumes in toil to soar
   To where Evangeline's memory clings,—

Such sights and sounds swift came and went,—
   Glad sunshafts of an April day!
And to impetuous traffic lent
   The restful sweetness of the may.

Imprisoned close in city marts,
   O childhood, so divinely fair,
For thee, deep in my heart of hearts,
   Sweet pity beats her wings all bare!

BAY OF FUNDY.

DEEP Bay, broad-breasted and brave!
 Oft rocked in thy swaying arms
 Beneath the hidden sun,
As foam-bell tost on thy wave
 I drift again 'mid thy charms
 To sphinx-like Blomidon.

Why are thy glories untold?
 Thy cliffs of purple and red
 And crystal-veinëd rocks,
Thy hasting waters deep-rolled
 'Neath skies whose colors are spread
 With art that all art mocks;

Thy faltering ranks of white mist
    Flanking vast floods and vast ebbs—
    A mimicry of war,—
Oriflammes of dew-sprent list,
    Banners of gossamer webs,
    Soft blown as lights of Thor !

II.

The smooth shining flats all bare
    To the heavens' nakedest ken,
    Mirror the hills, like lakes.
The drowsy lull of the air
    Will stir anew to life when
    The tidal note awakes.

From lang'rous south seas that creep,
    These odors dank issue forth,
    Odors of sun-steeped brine—
It comes ! a breeze from a deep,
    Full-fed from seas of the North,
    A waft of Vikings' wine !

Now beats the pulse of the flood,
    The throbbings deep of a heart
    Felt all around the world ;

Now smites its rhythm with a thud,
 With ictus sure of its art
 That mountains huge has hurled.

The unsouled rivers and creeks
 Have being, have life to the full,
 Into their mouths rebreathed,
As heaves the broad breast that seeks
 T' embosom each leaning hull,
 Bare on red banks tide-seethed.

The iron gride of the flow
 Powders the rocks in its path,
 And bears the dust afar
To build their urns, where may grow
 Sweet grasses and " primrose rathe,"—
 Fair Grand Pré, Tantramar !

III.

Builder, unbuilder of shores,
 Thresher of cliffs vapor-stoled,
 God's masterworkman strong !
Yet on thy bosom the oars
 Of sailor lads ply and fold
 To sweet refrains of song.

And glad in thy twinkling smiles,
   Awing, like sea-gulls, the ships
   Are breasting stout the breeze,—
Ah me, thy treacherous wiles !
   Witching fog-wraiths draping rips !
   Currents of iron seas !

IV.

O Fundy, deep-breathing sea,
   Regal in power and rimmed
   In hollow of His hand,
Captive to beauty, yet free,
   Sleep now, thy Basin is brimmed
   In fair Acadian land !

Haloed with pearl-raying rings
   The moon, at her utmost poised,
   Looks on her silver shield ;
And the tide wakens and swings—
   Ebbs with a clangor far noised
   And wheeling wings afield.

AT THE LOOK-OFF.

(PARTRIDGE ISLAND.)

I.

WHAT more can world-worn spirit ask
Than here in nature's arms to bask
And see the plangent tide at task?

The zest is swift as lusty youth,
(Touched with an undertone of ruth,)
Invincible as ageless truth,—

The wonder of all wondrous things!
How coy the birds! they lift their wings;
The wary ship to her anchor swings.

II.

Sun, moon and stars of ancient prime,
And of to-day, in confluence chime
The universal One sublime;

Pouring these floods of deep surcease,—
In universal pain, release;
In universal travail, peace.

The strong right arm is here laid bare
In strife, by which He doth declare
Another shall not with Him share.

Forces of universal law
Which hither these vast waters draw
Send through my soul His tides of awe;

While universal radiance charms
And beckons to His winsome arms
To soothe my timid soul's alarms.

Of joy, of grief He does not rob,—
The light with intermittent throb
Falls on the waters glad—a-sob.

III.

Here He and I are conscious each
Of each—a Deep, a waiting beach!
A shell, a Sea that doth beseech!

How all unswift my eyes to see
The universal God in Thee,
Who walked the waves of Galilee!

Give, freely give—Thou dost not dole!
Pour chrismal balm upon my soul!
Anoint me from Thy golden bowl!

IV.

In travail, pain, grief, joy, the wave
Slumbers nor sleeps the earth to save—
This word the blissful God He gave,

Ere yesterday in Palestine
Love's flagon poured the ruddy wine,
Life of the universal Vine.

V.

The tameless tides, unresting, seethe ;
I rest me, for He works beneath ;
Peace ! peace ! the toiling waters breathe.

Peace, healing peace, in murmuring main,
In brooding sky fanned by lone crane !
The sunbeams bicker in the Lane—

Peace on the lighter's falling sail !
Peace on the ships that breast the gale !
And peace in human hearts that fail !

THE STORMY PETREL.

FAIR hero, brave hero of sea—
   The sea in its darkness of wrath !
I run down the breaker with thee,
   I mount the next in its path.

Our hearts beat together, charmed one,
   Lift their wings as fearless as free,
Ride the gloom as if 'twere the sun
   Gold-bridled for you and for me.

Summer rain, the cold drifting sleet
   That whistles as spiteful as hail !
A roadstead, the billows that fleet
   Under the black lash of the gale !

We laugh at their seething, their roar,
   Draw our breath full in their face ;
We have wings, we know we can soar,—
   Your secret and mine in embrace !

(Wings, wings, the soul of our life !
   Outspread they victory tell,—
Upliftings amid gulfs of strife,
   Wafts of heaven that keep us from hell !)

Brave hero, winged hero of sea—
   The sea with black tempest in breast,
Here we mount on the breakers, free,
   Soon to soar into calm, into rest !

OBLIVION.

THE all-devouring sea ! I said,—
While looking on the green- and red-
Ribbed rocks a-tilt that flank Sharp's Head :

The diary of the rain cloud driven
To yield again its spoil by heaven,
The west wind serving the replevin—

Notes of the ocean's teeming floor,
The carven shell, the seaweed's spore,
And ripple-marks of tidal shore—

Vast tablets of the world of eld,
A mighty Bodleian unspelled,
By ravine into dust compelled!

The hills are fated to their fall.
Upon the great, upon the small,
Oblivion drops her raven pall.

II.

And then I thought: The form and mass
May baffle ken of eye and glass,
And yet the record may not pass.

Tittle and jot, where all seems nil,
A finer form in form may still
Wait touch of that which doth fulfil.

III.

The liquid air, unseen, unheard,
Writes in an everlasting word
The wing-beats of the hasting bird.

The sweet light leaves, and bears
    abroad,
A picture of the wide realms trod
With wingëd feet gold sandal-shod ;

Etching in truth and beauty's grace,
Beyond compare of antique vase,
On fronting hills the other's face.

Nor shoreless deeps of space debar
Blazon on earth of records far,
In greening orb or burning star.

IV.

I said : Coined for exchange in mart
Of purblind men with leaden heart,
This word Oblivion on life's chart !

Deft science' balance now prevails—
This simulacrum in the scales,
The verdict to the counter nails.

v.

And then, distraught by onward sweep
Of meditation long and deep,
I sought me out a place to weep—

O soul, may not thy leaves, I mused,
Stirred by death's shock through all diffused,
Reveal thy story unconfused,

Clear traced by thought's all-subtle beam—
A quickened palimpsest agleam,
Re-orient out of dusk and dream !

SEA MUSIC.

(For dramatic orchestration.)

I.

FLEECY white waters,
Shorn by the tempest,
Wrathful and doomful
Rolling to land !

Naked and lustrous,
Fiercest of smiters,
Straight for the stern cliffs,
Iron to steel !

126

Shock unto shock calls,
Boom answers boom,
Roars the huge tide-loom,
Thunder and storm !

Torn are the vast webs
Woven of tumult,
Flung to the cloud-rack,
Tatters of sound !

II.

The glistening waters again
Are marching loyal and true
Under the hollow sky,—
A hundred million of men
Throbbing as fiery dew
Under the morning's eye !

List to the repetend note,
Multiplex tone of the sea,
Refrain of grief, of mirth,

SEA MUSIC.

On violet air afloat
 Far borne to mountain and lea,
  To the home of its birth.

List as its music unbraids :—
 Rivulets pour from the hill,
  Winds wash the lips o' the trees,
The brook by the rocky glades
 Brattles its way to the mill
  Through fields adream with bees.

Forests of pine and of fir
 Plain as their dark plumes are fret
  By the free-coursing winds ;
Alder and golden birch stir
 To notes too sweet to forget,
  Sung by brook as it winds.

Hark ! *The lone laugh of the auk*
 As 'twere a disprisoned soul come
  From out the shining foams !
And the loon's " ha ! ha !" and mock
 'Mid the torn surf's booming drum,
  Or hushed tide's star-sprent domes !

SEA MUSIC.

The ringdove coos in the grove,
  The cataract's thunders jar,
    Rapids swirl white and hiss ;
Peoples in temples of love
  Echo their anthems afar,
    Diapasons of bliss.

Great flux of the world, O sea,
  Blood of earth's wild pulsing veins
    Beating to orbs afar,
Your life and mine cannot be
  Unlinked with God's joys and pains
    Here or in throbbing star !

List as its music unbraids,
List to the much-sounding sea,
List to the repetend note,
  Multiplex tone of the sea,—
    Refrain of grief, of mirth,
On violet air afloat
  Far borne to mountain and lea,
    To the home of its birth.

SUMMER FOG.

I.

Waft of beaten brine of the Bay,
  Tonic keen as steel in strife,
Blowing wet and cool in my face,
  Tang of bitter savor of life!

II.

Billows calm of whitest fog,
  Over ships and homes now roll,—
Breath of seas in quest of heaven,
  Groping blind as human soul,
Blearing, hiding, muffling all,—
  Life itself laid under the shroud!

III.

Breath-blown veils of faltering mist,
  Filmy dreams of luminous cloud,
Shifting curtains fret with air,
  Noiseless sped as northern lights ;
Opening, shutting gaps of blue,
  Gleams and glories, glooms and nights !

Torn by winds and riven in spray,
  Borne afar o'er pine trees tall,
Clinging round the mountain crests,
  Melt in azure roofing all !

IV.

Mystic phantom, mime of life :
  Witching visions, vanishing play,
Belts of shadow, rending veils,
  Cloudless dome of perfect day !

V.

Come again, white vapor of seas,
  Blow thy pungent balm in my face,
Soft illusions weave o'er earth,
  Charm me up to heaven's embrace !

THE ARETHUSA.

A PEARLY boat am I,
  From Silver Crag I hail,
Wrought of the sea and sky,
  Freighted with moonbeams pale.

I hoist my purple sails
  To catch the starbeam's gold,
And furl them in the gales
  The sun blows overbold.

Rainbows and flying tints,
  The sunset's crimson glow,
A thousand gleams and glints
  All day do come and go.

But as the silver moon
   Rolls up the breathless blue,
And all the stars in swoon
   Are hidden from my view,

I ope my hatches wide
   And lade with pearl and sheen,
To deck my home-bound bride,
   The Basin's peerless queen.

DIAN AND FUNDY.

(DESIGNS FOR A TIME-PIECE.)

I.

The Enchantress.

IN silver shoon, on sapphire pavement clear,
    Fair Dian walks the overarching night;
Her spell she lays—great Fundy leaps with cheer!
    She breaks—he flees in elemental might!

II.

The Lovers.

Dian, pale Dian, sailing the upper sea,
    Searching for lover lost on earth's lone beach;
And Fundy, forward, backward, ceaselessly,
    By love's impulsions borne to utmost reach.

III.

Art and Science.

Dian, with silver robe from her shoulders flung,
    And Fundy, with his tidal arc and gauge,
Beating as a great pendulum forth-swung,
    The seconds of the geologic age.

THE OLD FISHER'S SONG.

FROM the broad-shouldered Cobequids we saw
Prone Blomidon in lotos-eyed repose,
The immemorial vigil lapst to dream.
The Basin lay as if in calm of swoon.
Upon the bosom of the breathing tide
The drifting ships, wide-winged in air, in sea,
Sailed double on a single keel—a ship
In either stilly heaven, above, beneath.
The day was warm, and as we lay beside
The woodland brook and watched the pinfish play,
We saw the sky within a silver pool,
Like a great vase of lapis lazuli
Veined with the feathery spray of cirrus cloud,

While cumuli in spotless beauty bloomed
Therein—a garden of the gods! And all
The pool seemed fragrant with a myriad sweets.

"There's promise of fair morrow," Harold said,
"The witness of the sea and wood is one:
The hissing brine, moonstruck, comes vengeful up
Its iron gateways with remorseless flood—
This little brook in rage and foam tears through
A hundred hills—each sets a mirror at
Our feet of beauty's self.   And so, I ween,
The fury of the age will end as full
Of calm as are this sea and pool of heaven."

And breasting an old path to the carved shore
Where fell at ebb the sea-green billows clear,—
A path o'ertangled thick with alder hung
With tags that take the rich brown Vandyke loved,
And cool with dusky air in which, all still,
Eye-bright and fronded fern and lichened spruce
Swam deep in voiceless sea of wildwood balm—
My eye had sight of emerald moss and bells
That wreathed the bearded rocks that once were fire.

" Ho ! here is where the fisher lives who sings
All day while fingering nets, and chants the tide
To sleep," cried Harold, "as he tends his seines
At night. Some three-score souls like his would make
A state, and one such state the golden age.
This old man never knows when spring is past,
But pipes a robin song from May to May,
A fresh-blown breezy song of coming good—
He's piping now !"

> *Heirs of the century,*
>   *Sons of the next,*
> *Hearten your spirits,*
>   *Your souls keep unvext.*
> *There's an ebb in the tide,*
> *There's an open sea wide,*
>   *But where sun and star dart,*
>   *You've a trustworthy chart.*

      Beside the wave-worn cliffs,
Painted with rainbows of a thousand storms,
We sat us down, and took on grateful cheek
And brow the waking winds that yestermorn,
Far out Atlantic's grey unresting wastes,

In awful tempest smote the full-winged ship
And pluckt it naked to the hungry deep.
" Peace is of conflict born," I said, "and good
Seems rooted oft in ill.   Man gropes in fog,
And is a child tost in a cockle-shell.
The stars wink over him and then are gone,
The sun is not, and when he deems he's lost,
The shore breaks forth in silver welcome sweet."

> *Care for the coming man,*
>   *Heirs of the race,*
> *Hearten your spirits,*
>   *Gird ! quicken your pace !*
> *There's a sound in the air,*
> *There are trumpets ablare,*
>   *But there's nothing to dread,*
>   *You've God overhead.*

" The Sirens once were symbol of chief fears
That met the hardy mariner on life's main,"
Said Harold, musingly, " but now the coast
Is set with sirens groaning lest he touch
The isles mist-veiled and hooded white with fog,
But cruel as the Sisters twain of death.
Science, to-day, the witchery of the past

K   139

Turns into truth to guide the course of man,
Tracks to its lair disease, and bolt and flame
Subdues to service of the struggling race;
While breeze of health begins to fan alike
The cheeks of rich and poor in city ways,
And wisdom cries aloud in every street."

> *You of the world-ages,*
> *Saviors of man,*
> *Hearten your spirits,*
> *Lay open God's plan.*
> *Labor hungers and wastes*
> *While love tarries nor hastes,*
> *Yet the note's round and clear,*
> *The full time draweth near.*

"But what of man's grim lust and greed?" said I.
"The comradeship of stars and night is not
More awful than is that of man with sin,
Nor shows more steadfast purpose 'gainst the light.
The sky and air fresh-washed with summer rain
Forthwith begin to cloud with haze and smoke
Till smit again with lightning's wrath, and torn
By buffet of the thunder's pealing voice.
So hath it been with man, till judgment-ire

Reddens in vain to purge his murky sky
And flash the light of God upon his soul.
The beastly lure of drunkenness that cloaks
Itself in the white mantle of the Christ;
Delusion's wand that prints mirage for sight
On eyes of civic crowds, and nations, too,
Or, unclean, faith assoils in simple hearts;
The simpering guile that toys with capital
And robs the workman of his honest wage,
While like the surgy murmurs of the sea
Sounds out the moan of willing labor's voice
For bread to fill its famished children's mouths;
The lust of power to sit in place of God
And turn for selfish ends the wheels of fate
Of fellowman,—these wait a day of doom!"

Heirs of the century,
    Sons of renown,
Lift up humanity's
    Broad kingdom and crown.
There's a purpose replete,
To put all 'neath man's feet,
    And we see it begun
    In the Virgin's crowned Son.

141

" Injustice," Harold said, with eye that burned
Like a star, "*is* the devil's own trade-mark,
And hottest comes from hell through saintly hands !
The race of man is in the making yet.
Hypocrisy still deftly apes true worth—
Thus prophesying universal good.
Nature is non-committal of her end,
But God is hiding not man's destiny.
Yon fitful beacon flares the dark night through,
And then the kindling clouds, day's heralds, burn
In golden dawn.   Earth's skyward crags, which thirst
For news from God, are bathed in heavenly light,
And from their sunrise shoulders the full morn
Shoots far the splendors of its coming noon.
The shadows of a fleeing night yet dim
The age and mask a hundred ills as good,
More eager graspt at since they haste away ;
But from the slopes there pours a clear new light,
Divinely aired, above that of the sun.
Philosophy of schools, nor science wise,
Nor labor, of itself, life's secret finds,
That fills the promise of man's vermeil bloom.
'Tis love alone can sheathe the alien sword,
And crown mankind in his own kingdom lord."

Heirs of the coming age,
Makers of man,
The Christ be your pattern,
Ay, choose with elan.
There's a presence at hand,
There's a voice of command—
It is Love, King of men,
Alleluia, Amen!

And as we turned toward home by open beach,
The waves were loud in clamor on the shore ;
But over all, and far away, we caught
The drifting chant of the old Christian seer :

It is Love, King of men,
Alleluia, Amen!

NORA LEE.

I.

Away from Howth into the south
A stanch brave ship left harbor-mouth.

The *Easter Bell*, all sails a-swell,
Gallantly swept to sea they tell,

And Nora flamed like one ashamed,
When her fair sailor-man they named.

II.

Three moons did heap the cresting deep
Since Nora Lee was wed at Dreep.

144

Up from the dim grey ocean's rim
No tidings came of ship, or him.

A sea-gull's wing would make her sing,
And eye with smiles her wedding-ring.

If signal high flew in the sky,
She knew the *Easter Bell* was nigh,

And pulled a rose, as wife that knows
Her good man cometh at the close.

The white ship came—'twas not the name !
And Nora Lee was not the same.

III.

The kraken grim, in dream, did swim
Beside the *Easter Bell*, and him.

The ocean swell and harbor bell
Chimed in an endless passing knell.

In gleaming green of breaker's sheen,
The pallid light of death was seen.

145

NORA LEE.

The shaping clouds, the mist, like shrouds,
Floated in ever-thickening crowds,—

Till piping wind her blood did bind,
Froze by the phantoms of the mind.

IV.

"Cheer up, good wife," the neighbors rife
Said all, "the *Bell* has charmëd life.

"Brave Captain Head, no dawn a-red
In vain e'er signaled him, 'tis said.

"Of all this town, from foot to crown
No sailor has so just renown.

"The winds that blow, the reefs that grow,
Each one by heart he'd know, he'd know.

"Some night full soon, or morn, or noon,
The *Bell* will fly her home gossoon ! "

146

V.

The days they came and went the same,
The moons, the tides, the mists, the flame.

And Nora said : "Since I was wed
Six moons the heaping tides have led.

" In gloom I pine—(love makes him mine,
Alive or dead)— I'll throw the line !"

VI.

She pulled a rose, as wife that knows
Her good man cometh at the close.

Three neighbors true with her she drew
To the grey shore, and, calling, threw,

With passionate leap, far to the deep,
The life-line good wives always keep—

"O Mike, my man, my dear good man !
The line, the line, my dear good man !"

147

(Calling so sore adown the shore,
As fell the wintry surge's roar.)

Across the line of foaming brine,
Low answer came that lit her eyne.

.   .   .   .

The neighbors three with Nora Lee
All heard the words from out the sea,

Yet none e'er said what past the wed,—
A fearsome awe o'er them was spread.

VII.

When next moon fell, the *Easter Bell*
Sailed into harbor, as they tell,

With silk "gossoon" astream aboon—
And Nora in her calm did croon,

And softly tell: "I knew it well,
His head it tosseth with weed and shell."

TO W.

TO W.

"Neural and hæmal arch," you say,
"Tell out man's history to-day,
Brain and mechanics have their way."

Is structure then sole test of kin?
The ape from man, in form and skin,
Is far as holiness from sin!

Emotion swears with hand uplift,
That beauty is no mere makeshift,
Significance divine its drift.

Beauty of sound, articulate speech,
Lories and pyes might simians teach,
These, therefore, nearer to man reach ;

While nightingale and mocking-bird,
Approach, in music's heavenly word,
Closer than mammal e'er conferred.

II.

Were structure and function parallel,
The word might break the mystic spell,
But function doth its test compel.

Upward to man the beaver deft
In structure gains of tail bereft—
But if there were no house-skill left !—

And if in structure beavers be
In tooth and larynx nearer me
Than flirting blackbird in ash-tree,

His song beyond all such control
Comes up in kindred echo-roll,
With those that tremble in my soul.

III.

True, in mechanics there is seen
A gross resemblance in the mien
Of ape and man—thought nigh unclean !

But grosser want of function's shewn
Of human attribute and tone,—
Sweet rhythmic utterance unknown ;

Beauty of form, proportion fair,
And dignity—all wanting there,
Though neural and hæmal arch compare !

IV.

Of structure, all you find is that
A function it performs, whereat
A thus or thus of sight's come at.

And yet you truly know far more—
Feeling from out her open door
Affirms, in speech of beauty's lore :

"O, awesome !" "beauteous !" "pleasant
  too !"
" Inspiriting !" "ennobling !" " true !"
Or contrariwise—each as is due.

But no account of this you take :
Your thoughts are polarized, and make
An open sea of a tiny lake.

v.

You don't believe the colors of birds
And insects are God's painted words
To please the master of His herds !

" Mere marks ancestral, once of use,
Now useless as an empty cruse—
Derived, but not designed," your truce.

Yet why such skilful pains bestow,
That colors *once* had use, to shew ?
Vain zeal, since that you cannot know.

Fruitless your words! Is it not plain,
"Designed" or not, like April rain,
The end achieved *is* man's high gain?

VI.

'Tis folly to attempt truth's goal
With logic got of half the soul,—
Truth will not have the half, but whole.

Beauty, God's gladness seen in time,
Lights up Truth's calm white face sublime
With radiance of the golden prime!

Shall you and I look down for light?
Nay, upward let us fix our sight,
Downward's the awful gulf of night.

MARIE DEPURE.

L

MARIE DEPURE.

Not with her outward eyes, but with her mind,
Her living soul, her faith,—for she was blind—
Marie Depure, with simple, loving heart,
Had seen the Christ, and chosen the good part.

She never thought with Milton, in his pride,
"Does God exact day labor, light denied?"
But gave her willing hands as one who saw,
Deftly to plait for use the yellow straw.

With humble workers of her craft she wrought
For daily bread, and Christ's great lesson taught,
That love the life far more than meat regards,
And body, more than raiment sweet with nards.

MARIE DEPURE.

For when the pastor, who, like John, had leaned
Upon the Master's breast, spoke words that yeaned
The pity of his heart for those that sit
In heathen night, nor know Christ's torch is lit;

Marie Depure, her soul winged like a dove
Eager to bear the news of light and love,
Gave of her humble toil more than they all,—
Since love makes willing answer to Love's call.

Amazed, the man of God to Marie said:
"Your gift is great, a part I take instead;"
But she, with sweet insistence, spake him, "Nay,
I'm richer far than those who see the day.

"These workers of the golden straw buy oil,
When darkness falls, that they may see to toil;
But I am blind, I need no oil for light,—
I give this love-lit lamp for darker night."

Marie Depure! A sweet and gracious beam
Speed from thy burning lamp, a Christ-like gleam,
To those who in the darkness sit, and some
Who, without serving, pray, "Thy Kingdom
       Come!"

"BY THE LOVE."

AN EASTER IDYLL.

"BY THE LOVE."

An Easter Idyll.

　　　　　Twelve months agone
The beauteous face, all white with pity as
A wave with foam, sank in the dusk of death.
Four summers and the wafture of the fifth
Had poured their cataract of gold far down
The shining shoulders of the seraph boy,
While love, a father's and a mother's, hung
Above its laughter like a thing divine.

O golden head that drifted down to death !
Sweet eye and voice by silence swift devoured !
Dawn's kiss upon the forehead of the day !

The fresh-blown surge of grief was stilled,
And halcyon hope her azure wings outspread
As all the hollow sky on Easter morn
Was, like a lily, filled with golden light.
Swift through the hush of death the thrill of life
Touched the still chords of the fair mother's heart,
And woke unquenchable desire to lay
White lilies from the darksome mother-earth
Upon the tomb, where circled, like a dove,
Her wingèd hopes,—the tomb where long ago
White angels watched the birth of Life anew.

Beside the lilied mound she lingered long.
Her rising soul pushed at the gates of death,
Till, like a creek from which the moon has drunk
The tide, they yawned empty and bare of hope.
All spectral grew her heart with tearless grief
As some sweet plot of lichens reft of rain.
"There are no angels now," she said, "to roll
The stone away. O that He now were here
To raise my dead, if 'tis not all a myth!"
And as she spoke she lift a bitter face
Into the eyes of the bright Easter day.

Not far away she saw a little child
Of scarce five years, and drawing near she knew
Him one who never felt a mother's kiss,—
Now sitting at the grave where one long month
Had slept his father,—kith nor kin bequeathed
The boy in the wide circle of the earth.
She knew that, rose and rosebud on one stem,
Father and child had crimsoned life with love,
And that the wind of death had snatched
The rose and left the unsheltered bud alone ;
Yet blinded by the night of her own grief
Scarce had she seen his golden day's eclipse.
Now swift she marked the tender mobile lips,
The spirit-light aglow in eye, on brow,
And the rare beauty of the noble face.

" Is your name Mary," fearlessly he asked,
" Who with the angels talked when the great stone
Was rolled away?—" " O no, dear child," she said,—
" Whom are you looking for ? "   With reverent mien,
Yet eager voice, " For Jesus," said the child.
" O Jesus is not here, my darling boy,
He's risen, you know."   " Yes," said the wistful face,

"BY THE LOVE."

" I've waited here all day for Him to come
And raise my father up.   I thought perhaps
He sent you, 'tis so late, to.bid me stay
A little—O 'tis never too late for
Jesus !" he said, and brushed away the tear ;
" He's sure to come, for 'tis the Rising-Day."

The woman stoopt to kiss the wondrous boy,
And sat beside him there upon the grave,
And sobbed like organ swept by the master's hand.

" What makes you cry ?—perhaps your father's here
To be raised up ? "   " No darling,—but my child."
He stroked the woman's hand : " Don't cry," he said,
" Jesus does not forget the Rising-Day,
He'll surely come and give to you your child
And me my father—He will come to-night.
I saw the two men who from Emmaus came,
Go by at early morn, and Jesus will
Meet them, and turn and this way come, as they
In wonder all about His dying talk,
And rising too.   The men will know Him not,
But I shall, and will call to Him to stop

And raise my father up." "How shall you know
Him, my dear boy?" she asked. "O by His smile,
And by the picture father shewed me once,
But" (with his hand upon his heaving breast)
"I'll know Him best by the love I keep in here."
"Shall you?" she said, "and are you sure you'll know
Your father?" "My own father!" said the boy,
With wondering voice, "I'll know him by the love,
And so will you your child. They will not look
The same, for Jesus did not, but they knew
Him by His love." And finer grew the face
As the fond lingering voice, in love's own tones,
Repeated : "And we'll know them by the love."

Moveless a moment, as the tide at full,
Her heart hung in a balance, and as its
Tremulous deeps swayed to the signs of heaven,
Its wave broke o'er the banks of self to life.

"Philip," she cried, and clasped him in her arms,
"Jesus has gone to heaven, and I am sent
By Him to take you to your father now.
Come!" With faith strong as is the noonday sight,

Instant the child clasped home her trembling hand,
And passed without the gates, nor backward lookt.
Silent he went, for expectation held
Him fast, and a great light was on her face.

Entering her home, she bade that food be given
The famished boy; and when the maid brought milk,
Honey and bread with broilëd fish, he said,
With exultation: "Now I know this is
The house—it's all here just the same, and He'll
Be here to-night."   With wingëd feet the wife
Sped up the stair to meet her husband's step,
And in a rapture told him all, and of
The wonder-heart below.   "Heaven, a fair child,
An angel boy, has sent our stone to roll
Away!   For us his vision is no less
Than for himself.   O husband, this is life's
Supremest hour for us!—'*I shall know him
By the love*,' sweetly he says."—"It shall be
So indeed!" cried the father's yearning heart.

As she returned, the child most eager said,
In a sweet voice half-sob, but full of hope,

"O wash my face and comb my hair, before
I see my father—'tis not too late yet?"
The touch of the ineffable child-trust
Pierced deep her heart, yet with assuring tones
The words fell: " Philip, come, let us now go
To him."

        The arras opened on a face
Noble and winsome sweet, though smiles were close
To tears.   As azure bird on mountain stream
Halts a brief moment on some jutting crag,
Ere as a flash of streaming light it cleaves
The dewy darkness of the trickling dell ;
So for a moment halted the sweet child,
Took one step forward, and then leapt into
The arms where death-shade once was deep as night,
But where commingling love now glads the gloom,
All lit by the sweet azure of the heart.
With head thrown back, and questioning eyes agaze :
"Father—you're—changed!" he said, "but by the
      love,
We know each other—by the love, the love!"
The father's heaving heart did echo sweet,
"The love, the love!"

"BY THE LOVE."

And nestling down upon
The manly breast, the curly head, soft-stroked,
And soothed with all the lullabies of love,
Was rocked, like harbored sail, to rest of sleep,
Lapt in the love which fed his simple faith,
And poured a golden Easter in the heart
Of her who groped in darkness 'mong the tombs.

NOTES.

NOTES.

Page 17. *and erst "rose noble" bore thy grace.*—The "rose noble," an ancient English gold coin, first minted by Edward III., was stamped with the figure of the rose.

19. *The phantom of the buried tide.*—This phenomenon is not infrequently seen in the evenings of the last of August or early September. It is caused by the condensation of the invisible vapor of the air resting on the dyked lands—the former sea-bed. As the condensed vapor lies close upon the ground, the illusion of a full sea is complete in the moonlight, the shore line and creeks being perfectly traced.

28. *The title deeds of these rich shores are thine.*—Geologists affirm that Partridge Island is older than the mainland, or than the other islands mentioned.

29. TENNYSON ROCK.—This rock is the pinnacle of Pinnacle Island (one of the Five Islands, Basin of Minas). The rock is solitary, and nearly two hundred feet high at low water,—a seated figure strongly resembling, as seen from the Basin, Lord Tennyson in his old age—with his cloak about him.

M   171

32. GLOOSCAP.—The divine man of the Micmac Indians. His home was on the shores of the Basin of Minas, particularly at Partridge Island, the Five Islands, and Blomidon. He sailed away "into the west," because of the wickedness of men and beasts, not to return till they should heed his voice. (See "Legends of the Micmacs," gathered by the late Rev. Silas Tertius Rand, D.D., LL.D , of Hantsport, Nova Scotia, and published by Wellesley College, Wellesley, Mass.)

40. DAY AND NIGHT.—The last three lines of the sonnet refer to the "afterglow," which often appears (at Minas Basin) from half an hour to an hour or more after the first sunset colors have entirely faded into dusk.

45. MAYFLOWER.—The *Trailing Arbutus*.

48. THE GHOST FLOWER.—The *monotropa uniflora*, —a true flower, not a fungus. It grows in the deep shadows, the entire flower and stalk being colorless and wax-like. It has white, wax-like bracts in place of green leaves. The cup nods, and stalk and flower together often form an interrogation point (which fact, it will be observed, determines the cast of the sonnet). The flower is widely known as the Ghost Flower, but is often called Indian Pipe.

52. MCMASTER UNIVERSITY.—Founded as a distinctively Christian university, by the late William McMaster, of Toronto, merchant, founder of the Bank of Commerce, and a member of the Senate of the Dominion of Canada.

54. *Areopagus . . . Furies.*—The sessions of the
Areopagus, the highest judicial court at Athens, were
held on Mars' Hill. The Cave of the Furies was
beneath the same rock.

66. *And shewed the prints of palfrey's shoe.*—These
tiny horse-shoe prints, many of them sharp and perfect
even to the nail-heads, may be seen in abundance on the
branches of any horse-chestnut tree.

82. *Had I two loaves of bread,*—Mohammed. *Or let
me die*—Wordsworth,—uttered in view of his emotion at
the sight of the rainbow.

84. THE DRAGONFLY.—The species of neuropterous
insects referred to in the poem deposit their eggs in
water. The grub lives at the bottom of the lake or
pond, creeping on the submerged parts of aquatic plants
and feeding on aquatic insects. When the final trans-
formation is about to take place, the body of the insect
becomes swollen until, lighter than the water, it rises to
the surface. As its skin dries, it splits at the back, and
the perfect insect comes forth, with body and wings quite
soft and moist. When dry, the wings expand, until
presently the insect spreads them, and soaring upwards,
begins to dart to and fro in the full enjoyment of its new
and wondrous life.

115. *The moon at her utmost poised.*—The moon is in
meridian at high water in the Bay of Fundy.

159. "BY THE LOVE": AN EASTER IDYLL.—The
story on which this poem is founded was published in
the *Congregationalist*, by Helen Strong Thompson, as a
true incident of the Easter of 1894.